LONG, LONG AGO

A First Book About the Past

By Michael Berenstain

A GOLDEN BOOK • NEW YORK

Western Publishing Company, Inc., Racine, Wisconsin 53404

Things are happening!

Things are happening all around the world, right now—today!

We can learn about these things on TV.

We can read about them in the newspaper.

But what happened before today?
What happened a year ago?
What happened long, long ago?

We can learn about long-ago things in books.

The people of long ago wrote things down. They wrote down what happened to them.

That is called **history**.

4

Who started to write things down?

Who made the first history?

Let's find out.

Let's pretend that **we** are going back in time, long, long ago!

5

Five thousand years ago, people lived on the banks of the river Nile in the land of Egypt.

These people, the Egyptians, were among the very first people who learned to write.

They drew pictures of things they wanted to remember. In time, these pictures became a written language. They were called **hieroglyphics.**

Most Egyptian writing tells of the pharaohs—the powerful kings of Egypt. The pharaohs had huge buildings and statues made for them.

The biggest buildings were the pyramids. These mountains of stone were the pharaohs' tombs. When they died, the pharaohs' bodies were wrapped in cloth and placed in the tombs.

The pharaohs' cloth-wrapped bodies are called **mummies.**

4,500 years ago

The pharaohs owned many slaves who worked for them. Among the slaves were tribes of people called the Hebrews.

The Hebrews were forced to work in Egypt, building temples and palaces for the pharaohs.

But the Hebrews had a great leader named
Moses. He led them out of Egypt, across the
desert, to freedom in the land now called Israel.
The story of the Hebrews is told in the Bible.

11

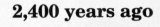

To the north of Egypt, across the sea, was the land of Greece. The Greeks were fine sailors. Their ships, called galleys, were powered by many oars as well as by sails. The Greeks painted eyes on their ships. Perhaps they believed this would help the ships "see" their way in fog or darkness.

Greece, Egypt, and many other lands were conquered by Rome—an Italian city that became the center of a great empire.

The Romans were famous soldiers.

They loved fighting so much that they even made a game of it.

Slaves called gladiators were forced to fight to the death in front of cheering crowds.

2,000 years ago

But the Romans were great builders, as well. Their cities were among the most splendid on earth.

And the Romans were great writers. They invented most of the alphabet we use today.

The Roman Empire lasted a long time. But it was finally destroyed by the barbarians—warrior tribes from the north.

This terrible time has been called the Dark Ages.

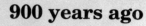

Europe was broken up into many different countries. These small kingdoms fought among themselves.

Rulers lived in strong castles to protect themselves. Knights in armor rode into battle. It was a time of almost constant war—the Middle Ages.

18

During the Middle Ages, the ancient lands of Asia were centers of learning.

The Arabs learned many things about the planets and the stars.

The Chinese made many inventions: paper money, the compass, and gunpowder, which was used to make fireworks.

Some of this learning reached Europe when travelers returned from the East. The new learning helped start a time of change. It was called the **Renaissance,** which means "rebirth."

The biggest change was in art. Artists began to create paintings that looked like real people.

New kinds of ships with better rigging were being built at this time. In 1492, Christopher Columbus used such ships to sail from Spain to America.

He was trying to reach China, but America was in his way.

No one in Europe had known about this vast New World.

There already were people living in America when Columbus arrived. He called them "Indians," because he thought he was in a part of the world called the Indies.

He was wrong.

People from Europe now came to live in America.

Settlers called Pilgrims went to North America from England. They arrived in winter. It was cold and there was little food. Friendly Indians helped them to hunt wild turkeys and, later, to plant corn.

After their first harvest, the Pilgrims held a feast—the very first Thanksgiving. They invited the Indians to join them.

More and more people traveled from England to North America. As time passed, they did not like the way the king of England was ruling over them.

They fought a war to create a new country all of their own: the United States of America.

Their leader was George Washington.
He commanded the army that fought against
the "redcoats"—the English soldiers.

Washington became the new country's
first President.

Americans began to move west, looking for new land. These pioneers often traveled in long groups of covered wagons called wagon trains. America was growing fast.

But America had a terrible problem.

In its southern states, people from Africa were sold into slavery.

Because of slavery, a war broke out between the North and the South—the Civil War. The North's leader was President Abraham Lincoln.

When the North won the war, the slaves were set free.

29

Then the world began to change very quickly. New inventions, such as the telephone and the automobile, changed the way people lived.

Scientists learned more and more about the world. Finally, they figured out a way to **leave** the world.

160-40 years ago

In 1969, a rocket carrying three American astronauts blasted off from earth. Its target was the moon!

For the first time in history, people walked on the surface of the moon.

22 years ago

And now we come to the very latest page in history . . .

31

today!

New history is happening right now!
But what will happen tomorrow?
What will happen in the future?
No one knows for sure.
But you can be a part of it.
You can make it happen!